Boats, Bo

by Sus

MW00946628

Table of Contents

Consultant: James R. Hipp, Ray S. Miller Army Airfield
Operations Officer, Minnesota Army National Guard, Camp Ripley

Boats Long Ago

People have always wanted to travel on the water. Boats let them do that. For thousands of years, people have been making new and better boats. Some are used for work. Some are just for fun!

Early Americans built **canoes** from tree bark and animal skins. They used paddles to move the canoes over the water. These canoes were strong enough to ride dangerous rivers.

model of Queen Anne's Revenge

A large boat is called a ship. One of the most famous pirate ships that sailed the seas was the *Queen Anne's Revenge*. A few years ago it was discovered at the bottom of the ocean.

About 150 years ago, riverboats carried supplies up and down our rivers. The boats were powered by big paddle wheels.

Boats at Work

This tugboat may be small but it's powerful. It's helping a large ship get into the harbor. The tugboat captain watches carefully as he steers the boat.

Fireboats put out fires on docks and on other ships. Often there is no other way to get water to these fires. Fireboats pump water up from the sea for their spray.

Look at all this ice! The sea is frozen and ships can't get through. That's why this **icebreaker** was called in to do its important job. It can break through very thick ice.

This **ferry** carries people and their cars across the water. People park their cars on the boat and enjoy the ride. Now they'll have their cars to drive on the other side!

Boats for Fun

People take vacations on huge **cruise ships**. Travelers can swim and watch movies on board.

These sailboats zip through the water as they race. The wind is the only thing that powers these boats. Sailboat racing is a popular sport.

A speedboat pulls this person as she rides a wakeboard. She holds on to a rope tied to the back of the boat. She flips, turns, and rolls in the air.

A **hydroplane** can reach racing speeds of 200 mph! (That's 320 kmph.) This type of boat moves just above the surface of the water. People like to watch hydroplane races.

Boats of Tomorrow

This boat is called the **Alvin**. It can dive down to the bottom of the ocean. People on the Alvin use robots to help them study the sea floor.

This boat was built to shoot movies underwater. It has cameras and lights on board. What other kinds of new boats do you think the future will bring?

Glossary

Alvin   a boat that can go to the bottom of the ocean and study the ocean floor

canoe   a light, narrow boat that moves by paddling

cruise ship   a large boat that takes people on vacations

ferry   a boat that regularly carries people and sometimes cars across the water

fireboat   a boat that puts out fires on the water

hydroplane   a fast boat that moves just above the surface of the water

icebreaker   a boat built to break up ocean ice so that ships can pass